Copyright © 1995 by Nord-Süd Verlag AG, Gossau Zürich, Switzerland
First published in Switzerland under the title *Holpeltolpel starker Freund*
English translation copyright © 1995 by North-South Books Inc.

First published in the United States, Great Britain, Canada,
Australia, and New Zealand in 1995 by North-South Books,
an imprint of Nord-Süd Verlag AG, Gossau Zürich, Switzerland.

Distributed in the United States by North-South Books Inc., New York.

Library of Congress Cataloging-in-Publication Data is available.
A CIP catalogue record for this book is available from The British Library.
ISBN 1-55858-397-1 (TRADE BINDING)
1 3 5 7 9 TB 10 8 6 4 2
ISBN 1-55858-398-X (LIBRARY BINDING)
1 3 5 7 9 LB 10 8 6 4 2
Printed in Belgium

Hermann Moers

Katie and the Big, Brave Bear

Illustrated by Józef Wilkoń

Translated by Marianne Martens

North-South Books

NEW YORK / LONDON

One day Katie's mother had to dash out to the supermarket to buy more milk. She told Katie she would be gone only for a few minutes, and reminded her that Mrs. Grant was right next door in case of an emergency.

As soon as Mother left, Katie was afraid. She imagined strange creatures lurking in the corners, waiting to get her, so she hid under the table with her book. It was a book about the biggest, bravest bear in the world.

Katie stared at the bear in the book. "I wish you were here right now to protect me," she said.

"Well, then, here I am!" said the big, brave bear, stretching up and out of the book.

Katie beamed. "Will you stay with me until Mother gets back?"

"I will indeed," said the bear. "Why don't we go to look for your mother? It was awfully stuffy in that book, and I could use some air. You'll have to help me, though," he added shyly. "I know very little about the world outside."

"Don't worry," said Katie. "I'll show you everything you need to know."

Katie put her hand in the bear's big paw as they left together. When they neared Mrs. Grant's door, Katie whispered, "Shhh! We have to be very quiet. Mrs. Grant is always complaining that I make too much noise on the stairs. She is very grouchy. I don't think she likes me."

"How can she not like you?" asked the bear. He tried to be quiet but his voice was loud and growly and his claws clicked as he walked down the hall.

Mrs. Grant threw open her door, an angry look on her face. Then she saw the big, brave bear. She turned as white as a sheet and slammed the door in terror.

Katie laughed, and she and the bear went clattering down the stairs.

Down on the street, Katie rode on the bear's shoulders. She wanted everyone to see her with her new friend.

The big, brave bear strolled along, not at all worried
by the people staring at them.

When they got to the supermarket, Katie looked at the heavy glass door with dismay. She could never open that!

"Allow me," said the bear. Carefully he took the door off its hinges and leaned it against the wall.

Inside, Katie searched anxiously for her mother. Finally she spotted her. Katie sighed with relief.

"It's okay," she said. "There she is, with her friend. They'll talk for ages. We might as well go exploring."

Back outside, the traffic was very heavy, with cars going this way and that, horns blaring. Katie was frightened. "How will we ever cross?" she asked.

"No problem," said the big, brave bear, and he sat down right in the middle of the street. All the cars stopped at once. When Katie had crossed safely, the bear lumbered calmly after her, then waved to the cars to be on their way.

Katie led the bear to a large construction site.
"This is where my father works," she told him.
"There he is, high up on the scaffolding." Katie
waved to her father.

"Oh, dear," she said. "How will he get
down—it's awfully high! It's a shame he
can't get a ride down on that crane."

The big, brave bear spat on his paws.
He picked up the crane and moved
it closer to the scaffolding.

Katie's father waved
his thanks. Then Katie
blew him a kiss
and waved
good-bye.

At the park, Katie saw an ice-cream seller napping on a bench. Just for fun, she put the ice-cream seller's hat on the bear's head. The bear jumped on the ice-cream seller's cart and rode happily around the park, ringing the bell as loudly as he could.

Luckily the bear got back to the bench just as the ice-cream seller was waking up.

"This fell off while you were asleep," said Katie, returning his hat.

They climbed to the top of the hill to look down on the park.

"Oh, no!" said Katie. "There's Charlie Rumbold. He's a big bully who's always pulling my hair!"

The big, brave bear grabbed Charlie and held him high in the air. "Pulling hair?" he growled. "That's not nice!"

Charlie trembled all over. "I'll never do it again! I promise!"

"Good," rumbled the bear. "Now, as a sign of peace, you two should rub noses with each other. It's an old bear custom."

"We really should get home," said Katie. "Mother will be worried if she gets back and I'm not there. We'll take the train—it's quicker."

The bear was thrilled with the station. "What a splendid cave this is!" he declared. "These rolling stairs are perfect for lazy bears."

With the big, brave bear holding her hand, Katie wasn't afraid of the long, scary escalator. Even the roar of the trains in the underground tunnels didn't frighten her today.

"There is one problem with this cave," said the bear. "I'm a sound sleeper, but those monsters on wheels make far too much noise. I don't want to be disturbed when I'm hibernating."

"Come along," said Katie with a smile. "It's not winter and there's no time to be lazy now."

When they got back home, they ran noisily up the stairs. Mrs. Grant didn't even open her door. They were still out of breath when Katie's mother came back. Katie ran to meet her.

"Mother! Mother! Come and meet my new friend. We've been out exploring the world!"

"Exploring the world?" Her mother looked confused.

Impatiently Katie led her mother down the hall to the living room.

"Now that I'm friends with the big, brave bear, I can do lots of things without you. I'm not afraid of anything when he's around."

As Katie and her mother came into the living room, the big, brave bear was already shrinking back into the book. Exploring with Katie had been great fun, and he was bearishly happy to have her for a friend. He couldn't wait until the next time Katie needed him. He would certainly be there for her.